Penny Dreadful is Incredibly Contagious

By Joanna Nadin

Illustrated by Jess Mikhail

P9-BBU-092

Contents

Penny Dreadful:
Boardroom Billionaire

page 97

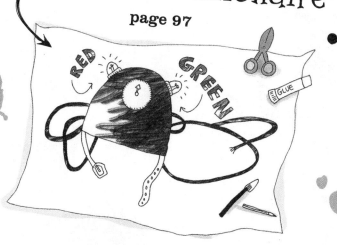

Meet Penny Dreadful and her Resigned Relations...

Penny
(It's never really her fault...)

Cosmo
(Penny's best friend)

Georgia May Morton-Jones
(Penny's genius cousin)

Daisy
(Penny's annoying sister)

Penny's long-suffering mom and dad

Very prim-and-proper **Aunt Deedee**

Barry
(Meow, I'm Gran's cat)

Gran
(Normally found fast asleep somewhere)

...her Crazy Classmates, and Sick and Tired Teachers

Bridget Grimes (Star Student)

Mr. Schumann (**SICK AND TIRED** principal)

Henry Potts (Cosmo's mortal enemy)

Sandwich fan, **Alexander Pringle**

Miss Patterson (Penny's tall-and-thin-like-a-beanpole teacher)

Shaves-his-head-every-week **rady O'Grady**

Cherry Scarpelli (Bridget's best-friend-forever)

Luke Bruce (Puts things up his nose)

Penny Dreadful

and the
Best Friend

My name is not actually Penny Dreadful.

It is Penelope Jones. The "Dreadful" part is my dad's **JOKE**. I know it is a joke because every time he says it he laughs like a honking goose. But I do not see the funny side.

9

Plus it is not even true that I am dreadful. It is like Gran says, i.e. that I am a **MAGNET FOR DISASTER**. Mom says if Gran kept a better eye on me in the first place instead of on *Zoomba Roomba* on FITTV then I might not be quite so magnetic. But Gran says if Mom wasn't so busy answering phones for Dr. Cement, who is her boss, and who has bulgy eyes like hard-boiled eggs (which is why everyone calls him Dr. Bugeye), and Dad wasn't so busy solving crises at the city council, then they would be able to solve some crises at
73 Rollins Road,
i.e. our house. So you
see it is completely
not my fault.

For instance, it is not my fault that Bridget Grimes is in **BIG TROUBLE** for toppling the model of the Leaning Tower of Pisa made entirely out of playing cards. It is because we are **VICTIMS OF CIRCUMSTANCE** (which means everything else that is happening in the world around you) and the **CIRCUMSTANCES** are:

a) A wasp

2. A factory that makes fish sticks

c) Miss Patterson's **GOLDEN OPPORTUNITY**

What happens is that I am on the corner of Newton Street trying to persuade a worm to climb on a pigeon feather (only the worm is not **INTO** the feather, he would rather climb on some mud), and also waiting for Cosmo Moon Webster (who is my best friend even though he is a week older and a boy) when his mom (who is called Sunflower, even though her real name is Barbara) comes out of her house completely quickly and **ALL OF A FLUSTER**. She says there has been an **ACCIDENT** and also an **INJURY** because Cosmo has been stung on the ear by a **WASP**,

because the wasp was not **INTO** wearing
a harness so it could pull a plastic tractor,
not even for a piece of toast and jelly.

And now Cosmo's ear is swollen and he cannot
hear and so he is not coming to school, he is
staying in his kitchen making a badge from
some raffia and four pipe
cleaners and **LOVE**,
because Sunflower
is very big on
things made with
LOVE, and also
natural fibers.

14

And almost immediately I am completely **GLOOMY** because I will have to sit all on my **OWN** at school, which means no whispering about stuff, e.g.:

1. What is better: chocolate or aliens?

2. Who would win in a fight between a monkey with a light saber and a crocodile with a sore foot?

c) Who can get a pencil to sit on their nose for the longest time?

(And it is me, although Miss Patterson, who is our teacher, and who is tall and thin like a beanpole, says it is not a **TRIUMPH FOR MANKIND**, it is **SHENANIGANS**, and if there is anymore I will be sent to see Mr. Schumann, the principal.)

4. Whether whispering counts as **SHENANIGANS**, which it turns out it does.

But when I get to school I am **DOUBLY** gloomy because Henry Potts, who is normally throwing erasers at Cosmo because he is his **MORTAL ENEMY**, is doing something else and it is saying Cosmo might **PERISH** from the wasp sting (if it was an especially stingy wasp) and then he will have to find a new **MORTAL ENEMY** and I will have to go around weeping in a black hat.

So then I am saying it is a **TRAGEDY** and **THE END OF THE WORLD** and maybe I am about to start weeping **RIGHT NOW**, only not in a black hat but in a red top and gray skirt, which is our uniform (even though Miss Patterson says it is not, because the skirt has purple pen on from where I tried to draw an ant, only it looked more like a train)

when I can completely hear that someone else is weeping but in proper uniform and it is Bridget Grimes, who is the star student in

our class and Mr. Schumann's favorite. And so I am wondering why she is weeping when she is not completely **INTO** Cosmo. And I think it is because either:

a) She has gotten a note wrong on the recorder, which almost **NEVER** happens.

18

2. Her long hair (which reaches her waist, and she is always swooshing and saying, "My hair reaches my  waist, Penelope Jones, and your hair is tangled with glue in it,") is tangled with glue in it, which almost **NEVER** happens.

c) Her mom and dad are actually international evil overlords who are trying to take over the world with an egg made of ectoplasm which takes away all your intelligence and she has to test the egg and will spell orangutan with a Q,

oraNgutaN
→ O

which is what Miss Patterson said I did. Only it wasn't a Q it was an O but my pen slipped because Henry Potts threw an eraser at Cosmo but it hit me by mistake.

Only it turns out it is none of them, not even **c)**, it is that Cherry Scarpelli (who is Bridget's best friend and who I have seen eat a crayon) has completely **GONE** to Grimsby because her dad is not going to be in charge of the golf ball factory anymore, he is going to be in charge of a fish stick factory.

And Bridget says it is a **TRAGEDY** and the **END OF THE WORLD** and worse than **PERISHING** from an extra-stingy wasp. And I say,

It is not.

And she says,

Is.

And I say,

Is not.

And she says,

Is.

And I am about to say, "*Is not is not is not*"
really fast so she cannot fit an "*Is*" in when
Miss Patterson fits something in, which is that
if she hears anymore about wasps
or fish sticks then she may very
well **PERISH** and that
instead she has an idea.
The idea is that I can sit
next to Bridget and we
can learn to be **FRIENDS**
and it will be good for
both of us and so it
is not a **TRAGEDY**,
it is a **GOLDEN
OPPORTUNITY**.

Only I do not think the opportunity is very **GOLDEN** because Bridget Grimes is normally always saying, "I would not do that if I were you, Penelope Jones." And Bridget doesn't think it is very **GOLDEN** because she says I have hit her three times this year with different things, i.e.:

a) A baked potato

2. An eraser in the shape of a snail

iii) A snail

Only I say the snail was supposed to hit Brady O'Grady but it bounced off the head of Alexander Pringle (who wears age 14 clothes even though he is nine) so it is completely not my fault. But Miss Patterson says that she will be the judge of what is **GOLDEN** and what is not and she judges that it **IS** so to sit down next to Bridget without anymore **KERFUFFLE** and think up four facts about horses.

And so I am sitting next to Bridget trying very hard to think about horses, only my brain is too busy thinking it is absolutely a **TRAGEDY** and the **END OF THE WORLD** and maybe I will have to run away to Finland or even Venus, when Bridget says she has already done three facts and they are:

1. Horses are taller than ponies.
2. Horses wear metal shoes.
3. French people eat horses.

And I say eating horses is not normal, and she says it *is* for French people, and I say French people are not normal, and she says I am not normal, and I say, "Am," and she says, "Are not," and I say, "Am," and she says, "Well do a fact then," and I say, "In fact, fact **4.** can be that horses cannot throw up."

And Bridget says she has **NEVER** seen *Animal SOS* and I say this is a **TRAGEDY** and also **THE END OF THE WORLD** and for once she agrees and so I am utterly **PLEASED AS PUNCH**. And so is Miss Patterson, because she says I have done **EXACTLY WHAT SHE ASKED** without breaking anything, throwing anything, or talking about vampires and I have shown myself to be a **PRIZE PUPIL** after all.

And for the rest of the week I am a **PRIZE PUPIL** a lot more times, e.g.:

1. I do not try to trade my orange for Brady O'Grady's chocolate graham cracker at lunch, not even by telling him it is a magic orange that will give him the power of turning into a toadstool – I eat it because it is completely full of vitamin C. Just like Bridget Grimes does.

2. I do not roll toilet paper around the hallway to leave a trail in case I get lost going

to Mr. Schumann's office and get eaten by a minotaur which is a beast with the head of a bull – I remember the way with my **BRAIN**. Just like Bridget Grimes does.

c) I do not poke Henry Potts with my ruler when he throws a pencil sharpener at me, I say, "I would not do that if I were you, Henry Potts, I would completely concentrate on my math so I am not a **MORON** when I grow up." Just like Bridget Grimes does.

And so I am **PLEASED AS PUNCH**. And so is Mr. Schumann, who says it is the first time he has not had to sort out a kerfuffle caused by me. And so is Mr. Eggs (who is the school janitor and smells like dogs), who says it is the first time he has not had to clean up a mess made by me. And so is Miss Patterson, who says it is evidence that the opportunity was definitely **GOLDEN** after all, because now I am sitting next to Bridget I am completely not a **MENACE** or a **MAGNET FOR DISASTER**, I am **MARVELOUS** and maybe we can be friends after all.

30

And I say this is a

 **BRILLIANT IDEA™**

because then we can watch *Animal SOS*

together. And Bridget Grimes says this is a

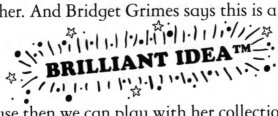 **BRILLIANT IDEA™**

because then we can play with her collection

of dolls in costumes from different countries.

And Mrs. Grimes says this is a

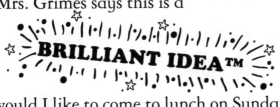 **BRILLIANT IDEA™**

and would I like to come to lunch on Sunday

and do both? And I say yes please and so it is

decided.

But on Sunday morning one person does not agree and that is Mom. She says the idea is not **BRILLIANT**, it is a **RECIPE FOR DISASTER** and she is already **UP TO HERE** with **HOOPLA** because Daisy (who is my sister, and who is very irritating) has had an argument about ankle socks with Lucy B. Finnegan (who is her best friend and who once got her finger stuck in our bathroom sink drain) and now they are **NOT TALKING**.

And Dad has had an argument with Mr. Hobnob (who is his boss and who has hairy hands) about stoplights and they are **NOT TALKING**.

And Gran has had an argument with Barry (who is her cat, and who is mostly eating things he should not be eating) about whether he is allowed to eat a chocolate bonbon, and they are **NOT TALKING** (although Barry does not normally talk, he just watches television).

But I say there will not be any **HOOPLA** or even one bit of an **ARGUMENT**, we will be completely best friends, she will see. And I can tell Mom does not think she will see at all, but luckily that very second Barry eats another chocolate bonbon and Gran starts shouting and Mom has to go and sort it out and so I go completely quickly to Bridget Grimes's house before she can say **JACK ROBINSON** (even though I do not know why she might even say this as we do not know anyone named Jack Robinson, only Jack McGillicuddy).

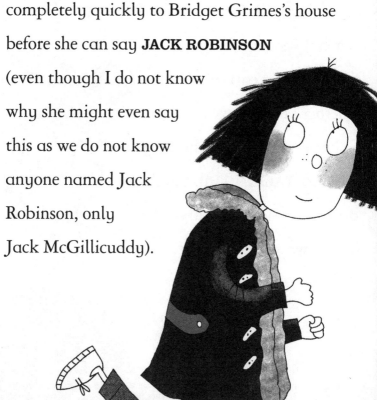

And I am right, because when I get to Bridget's there is absolutely no **HOOPLA**, there are grilled cheese sandwiches, and chocolate ice cream for dessert and we watch *Animal SOS* and this week it is a Labradoodle named Beryl, who has her paw stuck in the handle of a pair of scissors, and her owner, Norman Berenger, is worrying like **CRAZY**, but the vet does some sawing and we do "ooh"ing and "aah"ing and in the end Beryl is **FREE**, but Norman is not allowed to try to teach her to cut out paper shapes anymore.

And then I say I am completely **AMAZING** at cutting out paper shapes and I can make a whole chain of giraffes and Bridget says she is also **AMAZING** and can make a whole chain of **ELEPHANTS**, which are trickier than giraffes, and I am thinking they are not because giraffes are **SPINDLY** but I do not say so because I am a **BEST FRIEND**.

Anyway, we go at once to the study, which is where the scissors and the paper are, and also something else and it is a model of the Leaning Tower of Pisa made completely of playing cards. And then I am doing even more "ooh"ing and "aah"ing because it is the most **AMAZING** thing I have ever seen,

even better than:

a) A monkey stealing an ice cream and a sock, which was completely not my fault.

b) Alexander Pringle with his head stuck in the railings, which was completely not my fault.

3. My cousin Georgia May Morton-Jones with her head all shaved, which was completely not my fault.

And I say maybe I can make a paper giraffe to sit on the top of the leaning tower of playing cards,

but Bridget says **UNDER NO CIRCUMSTANCES** am I allowed to even **BREATHE** on the leaning tower of playing cards because it is Mr. Grimes's **PRIDE AND JOY** and if it topples over it will be a **TRAGEDY** and the **END OF THE WORLD** because he will not win the Tall Things Made Of Playing Cards competition.

And so we are cutting out giraffes and elephants, which is when I have my **BRILLIANT IDEA™** which is to invent a new animal that has an elephant nose and giraffe legs because then it will be a new and superior animal and will rule all animals in the world. But Bridget says we cannot just make up animals,

and I say,

Can.

And she says,

Cannot.

And I say,

Can.

Because once Cosmo made up
an animal that was half
cheetah and half shark and
half bee, and in fact it would
be the best animal in the world
because it would be able to run the fastest
underwater and also fly out when it was done.

Only Bridget says you cannot have three halves and I say, "Can *if I want*," and she says, "Cannot," and I say, "Can," and she says, "Cannot," and that is when the leaning tower of playing cards **ALL FALLS DOWN**.

And almost immediately Bridget is crying and saying we are in **BIG TROUBLE** and it is **ALL MY FAULT**.

But I say it is **NOT** my fault, it is that the tower is a **VICTIM OF CIRCUMSTANCES** and they are:

1. Some breathing.

b) A paper giraffe that was trying to attack a paper elephant, but my throw is **NOT AS GOOD AS IT MIGHT BE** and I know this because Miss Patterson says so because I have hit her on the head with a beanbag eleven times.

But I say there is no need to worry because as well as being **AMAZING** at cutting I am also **AMAZING** at building things with playing cards, and also glue.

And so we are gluing and sticking like **CRAZY** and we make a tower that is definitely very **TALL** and very **LEANING**, only Bridget says it does not look very Italian, which is where Pisa is, which I did not know, so I have learned a new thing and am a **PRIZE PUPIL** even on a Sunday.

I say it is because the tower does not have any spaghetti in it because spaghetti is from Italy. And so we go to the kitchen and we get some spaghetti, and the doll who is from Italy, and a marshmallow, which Bridget says is not Italian but I say it can be a cloud in the air, and we glue them all to the tower and I say "**TA-DAH**,"

which is when Mr. Grimes and Mrs. Grimes and a man who is named Alan and who is from the Tall Things Made Of Playing Cards competition all walk in.

And then there is very definitely **HOOPLA** and also an **ARGUMENT** and it is about glue and spaghetti and girls who even breathe on leaning things and Bridget is sent to her room to think about it and I am sent home to stay out of everyone's way.

Mom says it is **INEVITABLE** and Dad calls me Penny Dreadful and does the honking goose laugh, and Daisy says,

It is all your fault, Penelope Jones, you are such a complete **MORON**.

But I say I am not a **MORON**. I am a **VICTIM OF CIRCUMSTANCES**.

But on Monday something amazing has happened and it is that the **CIRCUMSTANCES** have completely changed because:

a) Cherry Scarpelli is not in Grimsby, she is back in her seat because her dad does not like being in charge of fish stick factories after all. He prefers golf balls.

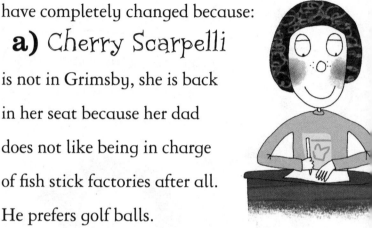

2. Cosmo Moon Webster is not at home making a badge with raffia

and pipe cleaners and **LOVE**, he is back in **HIS** seat because the extra-stingy wasp did not **PERISH** him after all.

So by ten o'clock we have been in trouble three times and Miss Patterson says it is a **TRAGEDY** and Mr. Schumann says it is the **END OF THE WORLD**.

But I say it is not, it is completely

BRILLIANT.

And Cosmo agrees, because he is my **BEST FRIEND**.

Penny Dreadful
Dreadful
is Incredibly Contagious

Normally I am not completely **INTO** going to school because of several things, i.e.:

1. Mr. Schumann, who is our principal, and who is mostly **SICK AND TIRED**, and it is quite often of me.

b) Bridget Grimes,  who is the star student in our class and Mr. Schumann's favorite, and who is mostly saying, *"I would not do that if I were you, Penelope Jones,"* only I do do it and she is right and it is very irritating.

3. Math, which is adding up numbers and taking away numbers to get another number,

only my number is mostly not the right number so I do not see the point.

But this week something **UNPRECEDENTED** happens which means it is completely new and has not happened before and it is **IMPETIGO**.

What happens is on Monday I find a small red dot on my chest and I think it is from where me and Cosmo were pretending to have been hit by the beams from laser-eyed dogs. Only the red dot does not wash off in the bathtub, which is where dots from laser-eyed dogs usually disappear.

It gets bigger and four more **PING** up all around it, which is totally **MYSTERIOUS**, and also itchy. And that is when I have my first

BRILLIANT IDEA™

which is that I will show them in show-and-tell and get a gold star for a **MYSTERIOUS** object because I have not gotten a single gold star this year even though I have brought in some very **MYSTERIOUS** objects, i.e.:

a) A gobstopper that I have sucked down to smaller than a pea.

b) A dead spider who has lost two legs.

3. An enormous egg.

So I go to **SHOW** Mom and also **TELL** her about the **MYSTERIOUS** and **ITCHY** dots which are maybe from an actual but invisible laser-eyed dog. Only Mom does not think it is from a dog, even one without laser eyes. And she also says this is not at all **MYSTERIOUS** but is very annoying because it means I cannot go to school for a whole week because

I am **INCREDIBLY CONTAGIOUS**.

Heaven knows who will take care of me because

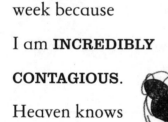

Dad is at a crucial conference on crosswalks and she is **UP TO HERE** with **HOOPLA** at Dr. Cement's what with all the boils. So Gran says it is fine, she can take care of me because she is not going to bingo at all until Arthur Peason says sorry about the cherry cake, which he says was dry and she says was **JUST RIGHT**. And I can tell Mom is not entirely happy about this because her lips go very thin. But as Gran says,

BEGGARS CAN'T BE CHOOSERS and so it is decided.

Only someone else is also not happy and that

is Daisy, who says it is **NOT FAIR** and why can't she have **IMPETIGO** or maybe **SCARLET FEVER** or **CONSUMPTION** and then she will not have to do double chemistry with Mr. Nubbin who smells like paint, and also George Helmet can sit at her bedside and cry for her. And then she finds a dot on her arm which she says is definitely **IMPETIGO**, only Mom says it is not, it is a **MOLE** and it is completely **NOT** contagious, and so it is chemistry for her, and anyway I will be bored by the end of the week and **BEGGING** to go back to

school. I say,

> Will not.

And Mom says,

> We'll see about that.

And I say,

> Let the seeing commence.

Because I am very **INTO**

things commencing.

61

And so on **DAY 1** I do not see because I have
a  **BRILLIANT IDEA™**, which is to build
a **RELAXING ROOM** from a giant cardboard

box that Barry likes to sit in, a cheese grater

and an odd sock.

And on **DAY 2** I do not see because I have a $\overset{\backslash\backslash|||||//||\backslash|||//}{\underset{/|\backslash|\backslash|\backslash|\backslash\backslash\backslash\backslash}{\textbf{BRILLIANT IDEA}^{\text{TM}}}}$ which is to make **MYSTERY** sandwiches, i.e. using everything from the pantry to find **UNPRECEDENTED** combinations, e.g. jam and cream cheese, which is very delicious, and also beets and peanut butter, which is not.

And on **DAY 3** I do not see because Gran has a
>))\|\|\|\|/\|\|/\|/
BRILLIANT IDEA™< which is to watch *Harper*
<///\|\|\|\'\|\|\|\\\\\
Fly, Girl Detective, which is a program on TV
where a normal sort of girl, e.g. like me, solves all
sorts of **MYSTERIOUS** mysteries with her **BRAIN**,
and a magnifying glass and a dog named Drew.

For instance, she solves:

a) Who has stolen all the birds in the world and it is the Caped Cahoot, her evil **MORTAL ENEMY**.

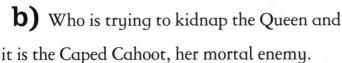

b) Who is trying to kidnap the Queen and it is the Caped Cahoot, her mortal enemy.

iii) Who has stolen the clock from Big Ben and amazingly it is not the Caped Cahoot, because he is scared of heights, it is his minion Horace McJigger, but the Caped Cahoot was the **MASTERMIND** and so he is still her **MORTAL ENEMY**.

But on **DAY 4** something else **UNPRECEDENTED** happens, which is that the TV completely **BLOWS UP**. What happens is that I am just

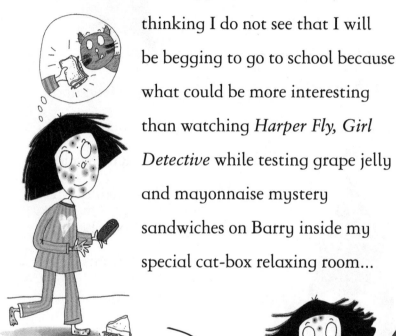

thinking I do not see that I will be begging to go to school because what could be more interesting than watching *Harper Fly, Girl Detective* while testing grape jelly and mayonnaise mystery sandwiches on Barry inside my special cat-box relaxing room...

when I slip on a mystery sandwich...

and trip over the cat-box relaxing room, and the remote control flies into the TV...

which goes **POP** and the picture wobbles and then goes **BLACK**...

And I say,

Oops.

And Gran says,

Uh-oh.

And Mom says a lot of things when she gets home from work, e.g.

Well there will be no TV until Mr. Beam can come and fix it, which is not until Monday.

And Dad says,

I can fix it. Did I ever tell you I could have been a TV repairman if I hadn't met your mother?

Only Mom says no he could not because he cannot even change channels without it going wrong and if he even thinks of going near the TV with a wrench then she might **BLOW UP** too. And Daisy says,

It is all your fault, Penelope Jones, you are such a **COMPLETE MORON**.

And I say I wish I was back at school after all, so in fact I do see.

And so on **DAY 5** I am completely **GLOOMY** because there is no TV because it is **BLOWN UP** and no cat-box relaxing room because it is all **SQUISHED** and no mystery sandwiches because Mom says they are **BANNED** and so it is fish sticks for lunch, which are not even one bit **MYSTERIOUS**.

And so after I have eaten my unmysterious
fish sticks I say I am so **BORED** I may well
PERISH or maybe instead I can just go into
town for a minute. But Gran says no I cannot
because I am still **INCREDIBLY CONTAGIOUS**
and I am not allowed to touch anyone for
even a second, **ESPECIALLY** not my
cousin Georgia May Morton-
Jones, because she has a
crucial ballet exam next
week and Miss
Pettifer says she
shows potential
with her pliés. And
so I am dangling off
the sofa and sighing

when I see a **MYSTERIOUS** object near the

baseboard and it is Daisy's tin of mints that

went missing last week

and she said

I had eaten them for

VENGEANCE and

I said Barry had eaten

them for **VENGEANCE** and Mom said if we did

not stop arguing she would ban mints forever for

VENGEANCE and so we stopped. But now I am

PLEASED AS PUNCH because I have completely

solved a mystery, which is when I have my next

BRILLIANT IDEA™, which is to become

a girl detective like Harper Fly. And so I

go completely quickly to my bedroom to

get my **ESSENTIAL EQUIPMENT,**

i.e. a magnifying glass, but not my **BRAIN** because it is in my head, or my dog named Drew because I do not have one yet. And then I write a list of all the unsolved **MYSTERIES** in our house and they are:

1. **WHICH** menace left the lid off the cookie jar **AGAIN**?

b) **WHO** drew the picture of a cat on the pantry?

iii) **WHEN** will kingdom come? (Because that is when I am allowed a dog named Drew, according to Mom.)

4. **WHERE** have all the odd socks gone?

And almost immediately I have solved **1.** and **b)** because I remember it was me after all. And I ask Gran when kingdom will come and she says Tuesday so that means **iii)** is solved too. And so it is just the missing socks and I use my magnifying glass and also my **BRAIN**, because Harper Fly says her brain is her most important tool, and I find eleven odd socks in **MYSTERIOUS PLACES**, e.g.:

a) Four in my underwear drawer.

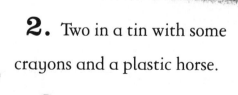

2. Two in a tin with some crayons and a plastic horse.

3. Three in my toy box from when Minimus Mayhem and two Herobots got cold and needed sleeping bags.

iv) One on my foot.

e) One in the squished cat-box relaxing room.

Which means
there is not actually
a sock-eating monkey
living under the
floorboards, which is what
Dad said and which I was quite **INTO**, but I do
not completely mind because it means I am the
best Girl Detective **EVER**, even better than
Harper Fly because she still hasn't found out who
the evil Caped Cahoot really is even though I
know it is her own Uncle Fester Fly and so it is
her **ULTIMATE MYSTERY**.

And I am just wondering what my **ULTIMATE
MYSTERY** can be, e.g. maybe my own dad is in
fact the evil Caped Cahoot, when the phone rings
and I **GASP** because I think it is possibly the

police calling to tell me they have arrested Dad for stealing the moon. Only it is not, it is Aunt Deedee calling to tell Mom that she is having problems with Georgia May Morton-Jones, who is not completely **INTO** ballet anymore, which is **OUT OF THE BLUE** and also very **IRRITATING** because of the exam and the pliés. And also can I actually pass on the message this time because last time she called to tell Mom about some cheese I forgot until a week later and so the cheese went bad. And so I say yes I absolutely promise I will tell her and thank you for calling, goodbye.

And then I **GASP** again because I have had another

which is that instead of telling Mom the message I will go to Georgia May Morton-Jones's ballet class, which is at the recreation center at three o'clock, and I will look very carefully at Georgia May with my magnifying glass and my **BRAIN** and I will solve the **MYSTERY** of why she is not completely **INTO** ballet anymore and it will be my **ULTIMATE MYSTERY** and I will definitely be the best Girl Detective in the World **EVER**.

Only then I remember that this is tricky because I am not allowed out because of being **INCREDIBLY CONTAGIOUS**, which means I am utterly **THWARTED** and full of **GLOOM** again. Only almost immediately I am **UNTHWARTED** because I remember that when Harper Fly had to solve a mystery at the opera she went in **DISGUISE**, i.e. in a red wig and a black ruffly dress and a pair of glasses, and so I will go to ballet in **DISGUISE** and it will be one that also covers up my spots so that no one will know I am contagious. Only it will not be a wig and a ruffly dress and a pair of glasses because I do not have any of those, it will be Daisy's cat costume and blue face paint, which will be completely **MYSTERIOUS** and so everyone will be **NONE THE WISER**.

And Gran is definitely **NONE THE WISER**, because when she sees me she screams because she has mistaken me for a **MADMAN**, and so she is going to have a nice nap on the couch and so I do not even have to ask permission to leave the house.

And lots of other people are **NONE THE WISER**, i.e.:

a) Arthur Peason, who is Gran's friend, who walks into a tree when he sees me.

2. Shaniqua Reynolds from the hair salon, who snips a bit too much off Mrs. Nugent's head when she sees me.

3. Mrs. Butterworth, who has a

mustache and a beady eye and who says,

GENERAL STORE

Penelope Jones is that you under that disguise?

when she sees me.

So I say,

No, it is Penelope Fly the **MYSTERY CAT**.

And she says,

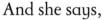

> Well stay out of the general store because I do not want any blue paint on the envelopes, not after last time.

And so I do stay out because I am already late for ballet and Miss Pettifer is not **INTO** lateness.

And it turns out she is not very **INTO** blue cats in her class either, because she says,

Cassandra Pickett, how many times have I told you that it is **PINK LEOTARDS** and **PINK LEOTARDS ONLY**? You will have to go to the back and if it happens again you will have to sit out, and color.

And so I am

PLEASED AS PUNCH,

because my disguise

has worked, because

she thinks I am

Cassandra Pickett.

And so I am at the back and I am doing
pliés and pointy toes while I watch Georgia
May with my **BRAIN**, but not my magnifying
glass because Miss Pettifer is not **INTO**
magnifying glasses either. And I notice
something very **MYSTERIOUS**, which is
that Tallulah Taylor-Hobbs,
who has a pony and
a cell phone
even though
she is only six,
is saying
something
to Georgia
May and
it is,

But I do not because I am jubilant because the **MYSTERY IS SOLVED** and it is that Tallulah Taylor-Hobbs is Georgia May's **MORTAL ENEMY** and is determined to **THWART** her. And that is when I have my next **BRILLIANT IDEA™,** which is that I have to **THWART** Tallulah Taylor-Hobbs back and the best way to do that is to lasso her with my cat tail. And so instead of doing a plié I do something else, but it is not a pointy toe, it is a pirouette, which is ballet talk for spinning around and I am **AMAZING** at spinning because I spin around three times and my tail is lassoing like **CRAZY**. And it completely lassoes Tallulah Taylor-Hobbs, who lands in a **HEAP** on the ground.

And so do several other people, e.g.:

a) Phoebe Patterson-Parry, who everyone knows has two left feet and both of them trip over Tallulah and so she lands in a **HEAP** on the ground.

b) Octavia Briggs, who trips over Phoebe Patterson-Parry and lands in a **HEAP** on the ground.

3. Miss Pettifer, who trips over Octavia Briggs and lands in a **HEAP** on the ground.

Which is when Aunt Deedee and Mom and Gran all walk in.

What has happened is
that Aunt Deedee has called
Mom at Dr. Cement's to ask
about the ballet **MYSTERY**
message and Mom says
no she has not gotten it
and she will ask me
when she gets home.

Only when she
gets home I am
MYSTERIOUSLY not
there, but Gran says
she is looking for the
wrong girl, i.e. I am
not Penelope Jones,
I am a blue-faced cat.

And then Arthur Peason has stopped by to ask Gran if she wants to go to bingo and he says he has seen a blue-faced cat walking toward the hair salon.

And Shaniqua Reynolds has said she has seen a blue-faced cat walking toward the general store.

And Mrs. Butterworth has said she has not seen a blue-faced cat but she has seen a blue-faced menace, i.e. Penelope Jones, i.e. me, heading for the recreation

center and she has also seen Aunt Deedee, who if you ask her drives far too fast. But Mom does not ask her, she just follows Aunt Deedee to the blue-faced cat who is also Penelope Jones, and then it is mystery solved because here I am.

Mom says I am banned from solving mysteries until **KINGDOM COME**. And Miss Pettifer says I am banned from ballet until **KINGDOM COME**. And Aunt Deedee says I am banned from everything until **KINGDOM COME**.

But I do not mind because Gran said **KINGDOM** will **COME** on Tuesday, and I think it definitely will because by Monday Aunt Deedee calls to say Georgia May has not gotten impetigo but she has passed her ballet exam so it is lucky for me. But it is not so lucky for Tallulah Taylor-Hobbs, who is **INCREDIBLY CONTAGIOUS** and cannot do even a plié.

Penny Dreadful:

Boardroom
Billionaire

I am
really **INTO**
television, even
though Mrs. Butterworth,
who works at the general
store and who has a mustache
and a beady eye and it is
mostly on me, says it will turn
my eyes square and shrink my
brain if I watch too much.

But I do not agree because I have checked and my eyes are definitely eye-shaped and my brain is not shrunk but is **BULGING** with ideas and it is all due to television.

This is because normally my favorite TV programs are:

1. *Animal SOS*, which is where animals almost die and then they don't and it is **MIRACULOUS**.

b) *Harper Fly, Girl Detective*, which is where a normal sort of girl, e.g. like me, solves

 all sorts of **MYSTERIOUS** mysteries with her brain and a magnifying glass and a dog named Drew.

But this week *Harper Fly, Girl Detective* was completely not there at all, which I say is the **END OF THE WORLD** and I might actually **PERISH**, but Gran says is a **GOOD** thing because it means *Boardroom Billionaire* is on instead and it is her third favorite show after horse racing and *Animal SOS*.

What happens on *Boardroom Billionaire* is that people have to **INVENT** amazing objects, e.g.

a toaster that can tell the time in five countries,

RING, RING!

or a watch that is also a telephone,

or a gizmo for picking up thingamajigs,

and then they try to sell them to the **EXECS**,
who are men in suits and a woman with very
red lipstick, who say,

Yes, it is
a **CLEVER**
invention, so it
goes **STRAIGHT
TO THE
BOARDROOM**

which is a room for people with **BUSINESS
BRAINS** and in the room is a pile of money to
make their invention in a factory and sell it in
stores. Or sometimes they say,

Are you **NUTS**?
This will never
work, please go
**BACK TO THE
DRAWING BOARD**.

So you see it is completely **AMAZING** and Cosmo agrees even though he does not have television because his mom, Sunflower, who is actually named Barbara, agrees with Mrs. Butterworth about the square eyes, which is a miracle because normally they do not agree on even one thing, e.g. Sunflower believes in **FREEDOM** and **SELF-EXPRESSION** and Mrs. Butterworth believes in keeping the general store ship-shape and rules. But Cosmo is going to do a **CAMPAIGN** to get a television, with a sit-in protest and banners, because Sunflower is very **INTO** sit-in protests and banners. But until then he comes to our house to watch TV and Sunflower cannot even say a thing because he says it is **SELF-EXPRESSION**.

So Cosmo is over at our house watching *Boardroom Billionaire* and this week it is a woman named Marjory Muldoon, who has invented a pair of slippers that are also a fire alarm. The execs cannot decide if it is **STRAIGHT TO THE BOARDROOM** or **BACK TO THE DRAWING BOARD** and so Marjory is a nervous wreck and so are me and Cosmo but in the end the execs agree it is **STRAIGHT TO THE BOARDROOM** and she gets a hundred thousand dollars and a factory in China.

Which is when I have my

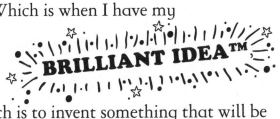

which is to invent something that will be

STRAIGHT TO THE BOARDROOM and

we will get a hundred
thousand dollars
and a factory and our
invention will be in every store, even
the general store, so Mrs. Butterworth will be **LOST
FOR WORDS** and so will Sunflower, and so will Mr.
Schumann our principal, and so will Bridget
Grimes, who is the star student in our class and Mr.
Schumann's favorite and who is normally never
lost for words and the words are, *"I would not do
that if I were you, Penelope Jones."*

And Cosmo agrees because he says it will be
COLLATERAL in his campaign for a television
set, and so we get a piece of paper, and a pen,
and our **UNSTUNTED** brains and we write a list
of inventions and they are:

a) A **TIME MACHINE**, because Cosmo is very **INTO** building time machines, especially ones made out of a bus, some tinfoil and an alarm clock.

b) A **PATENTED BRAIN EXPANDER HELMET**, which will massage your imagination while you are watching, say, *Animal SOS*, because it will be **MORE COLLATERAL** in Cosmo's campaign for a TV.

iii) A **MONEY-MAKING GADGET**, so that Mom will never say, "No, Penelope Jones, you may not go to Monkey Madness Safari Park because you still owe me $42.93 and also I only have five dollars in my purse and I need it for cheese."

4. A **MAGIC RADIO** that knows exactly what you want to listen to without you **FIDDLING WITH BUTTONS**, because Mom is always telling Dad to stop fiddling with buttons because they fall off, which means she has to listen to *Traffic Management Today* or nothing at all.

Only I do not think we can do the time machine because we have run out of tinfoil since the day I tried to go to school dressed as an airplane,

and also I am not sure where we will get a bus
from. And Daisy says we cannot make a
money-making gadget because it is against the
law to make actual money unless you are the
President and I will be
arrested and go to
prison, so I am a
complete **MORON**.

And Mom says no we cannot have the radio because Dad is listening to *Traffic Management Today* because he has a crucial meeting tomorrow with Mr. Hobnob (who is his boss and who has hairy hands), and also with Mr. O'Flannery (who is Mr. Hobnob's boss, and who I have never met so he might have even hairier hands for all I know). And so it is definitely the **PATENTED BRAIN MASSAGING HELMET** and it is a **BRILLIANT IDEA™** and it will be **STRAIGHT TO THE BOARDROOM** for a hundred thousand dollars.

But Cosmo says before we get to the **BOARDROOM** we have to start at the **DRAWING BOARD** and design our helmet.

So we get some paper and a pen that has four colors, only the black does not work from when I drew seventeen pictures of the sky at night in a row, and we do our design. And the design is **AMAZING** because it has lots of important wires and a dial on the front and a light that flashes red for when your brain is **STUNTED** and green for when your imagination is completely **MASSAGED**.

Only Daisy does not agree it is **AMAZING** because she is **KILLING** herself laughing and saying,

You are **CRAZY** if you think you can make a **PATENTED BRAIN MASSAGING HELMET**, you cannot even make a hat with a feather!

Which is true, but is because the feather would not stick onto the swimming cap and Mom would not let me have any glue for various reasons. And Mom does not agree it is **AMAZING** because she says she is **UP TO HERE**

what with Dad and his crucial meeting and so
the last thing she needs is two menaces making
dangerous hats in her kitchen and can we
please go to Cosmo's if we want to do anything
loud or messy or crazy. And so we do.

It is much easier to make **PATENTED BRAIN MASSAGING HELMETS** at Cosmo's because of the **FREEDOM** and **SELF-EXPRESSION** and also because the scissors are not in the **OFF LIMITS** drawer and nor is the glue or the tape or the batteries or the remote-controlled car. But we still do not have an actual helmet to stick all the stuff to and patent and do brain massaging with and so Cosmo says we need to **MAKE DO** with whatever is around us, because Sunflower is also very **INTO MAKING DO**. And so we look around us for things to **MAKE DO** with and we find:

a) A saucepan with some green soup in it.

2. A plastic policeman's hat with some worms in it.

iii) A dishwashing tub with some plates in it.

4. A plastic flowerpot with some dead daisies in it.

And Cosmo says it cannot be the saucepan because the soup is not eaten yet and it would be **WASTEFUL** and Sunflower is not **INTO** waste. And it cannot be the policeman's hat because the worms might be hibernating and waking them up would be **CRUELTY TO ANIMALS** and Sunflower is not **INTO** cruelty to animals. And it cannot be the dish-washing tub because that would mean doing the washing-up, which would be **CHILD LABOR** and Sunflower is not **INTO** child labor. So it is the plastic flowerpot, only we take the dead daisies out and put them in the compost bin, which is not wasteful, or cruel to animals, and only a tiny bit of **CHILD LABOR** so it is fine.

Then we glue on the remote-controlled car so that its wheels whiz on the plastic, which will do the massaging, and then we stick on some extra wire so that it looks **IMPORTANT** and **CONFUSING**, because execs like things that look important and confusing. Then we

 make a sign with purple marker that says "**PATENTED**" and has our **LOGO**, which is our special badge and which is actually supposed to be a winged lion killing a verminous beast, only it looks like it is a dead ant being licked by a bee because I cannot draw lions and Cosmo cannot draw verminous beasts, and then we stick it on the front and so it is **DONE**.

Only Cosmo says in fact it is **NOT** done because we have not **TESTED** it for efficiency, and the execs are very **INTO** testing for efficiency. Only we do not have a television to watch, so Cosmo says he will pretend to be Harper Fly while I wear the helmet and then I can pretend to be Harper Fly while he wears the helmet. And so I put the helmet on and press the button on the remote control and it is **AMAZING** because it is completely buzzy inside and I cannot hear what Cosmo is saying, but suddenly I remember that lions do not have stripes and so I think my brain has definitely **EXPANDED**.

And then Cosmo puts the helmet on and he says his brain has definitely **EXPANDED** too, because now he knows what seven times five is and it is thirty-five, not "*I do not care because math will not matter when I am Lord of the Dolphins*," which is what he told Mr. Schumann last week and which meant he had to sit at the back of the class and read a book about the Romans.

And I say, "*Hurray, it is a success because we are both* **SUPERIORLY INTELLIGENT** *so it is* **STRAIGHT TO THE BOARDROOM**."

But Cosmo says it is **NOT** because it has not been tested on **JOE PUBLIC**, which means everyone except us and the execs are very into things being tested on **JOE PUBLIC**. And so we decide to go into town and find **JOE PUBLIC**, and if not then Mrs. Butterworth from the general store will do, because her brain absolutely needs expanding so that it is not always being upset with me because her beady eye has seen me touch a mug with a picture of a cat on it, for instance.

But when we get to the general store, Mrs. Butterworth says she will absolutely **NOT** try the **PATENTED BRAIN MASSAGING HELMET** on because her brain does **NOT** need expanding and she will be reporting me to my mom for saying it does.

And Mr. Nutkins, who is buying twelve first-class stamps and three jars of pickles, will **NOT** try the **PATENTED BRAIN MASSAGING HELMET** on because it will not go over his hearing aid.

And Bridget Grimes, who is looking at rulers,

MUGS 6·95

RULERS 1·00

TAPE 50c   BUBBLE WRA

will **NOT** try the **PATENTED BRAIN MASSAGING HELMET** on, and says,

> I would not do that if I were you, Penelope Jones.

And then it is Cosmo's turn to have a **BRILLIANT IDEA™** which is that we need someone who is more **INTO** being **SUPERIORLY INTELLIGENT**, e.g. Aunt Deedee. And it is even clearer that the helmet has expanded his brain because

that is especially clever. And so we scoot to
Aunt Deedee's house, which is only four
streets away but it is very much bigger than
our house and also much cleaner because of
all the rules, e.g.:

1. No eating except at the table.
2. No clay or paint or glue
except at the table and only if it is
covered in a plastic cloth.
C. No eating clay or paint
or glue.

Plus if you even **LOOK** at a glass
candlestick Aunt Deedee says, "Do not
even think about it, Penelope Jones."

Only when we get there she will **NOT** try on the **PATENTED BRAIN MASSAGING HELMET**, and nor will Lilya Bobylev, the nanny, and nor will Georgia May Morton-Jones, even though Aunt Deedee says she has a brain the size of Einstein, who was a very **SUPERIORLY INTELLIGENT** person. So I say, but it will expand her brain even more, maybe even to

the size of Maximus Terror's, who is leader of the
Zombiebots and who knows how to melt an
army of metal monkeys with the tip of his finger,
and then she will get a hundred on her math test
and maybe even in Mandarin (which is not a
fruit, it is a language like Chinese). Only Aunt
Deedee says Georgia May already has a
hundred in math and Mandarin and she does
not want her to know how to melt an army of
metal monkeys with the tip of her finger. Plus,
if I even **THINK** of putting the helmet on Georgia
May while she is not
looking she
will have my
GUTS FOR
GARTERS

and frankly I will be lucky to persuade
anyone to try it on unless they have a brain
the size of a peanut.

Which is when I have another

BRILLIANT IDEA™

with my expanded brain, which is to go home
and get Mom to try it on, because she did not
say we could not **USE** the helmet in the house,
she just said we could not do anything
loud or messy or crazy, and the
helmet is definitely not messy or
crazy and is only a little bit loud,
but the TV will be louder,
and so it is decided
and we go home.

But when we get home Mom says no she will

NOT try the **PATENTED BRAIN MASSAGING**

HELMET on, because she is **UP TO HERE** with

HOOPLA because Daisy and Lucy B. Finnegan

are not hating each other anymore, they are in

the kitchen making cupcakes and also a mess,

and Dad's crucial meeting is this afternoon

only he has **LOST** a diagram and is turning the

house upside
down looking
for it.

And Gran says **SHE** will not try the **PATENTED BRAIN MASSAGING HELMET** on because she just had her hair done for bingo and Shaniqua Reynolds says she is not allowed to wear hats for twenty-four hours or the curls will wilt.

And Daisy and Lucy B. Finnegan say **THEY** will not try the **PATENTED BRAIN MASSAGING HELMET** on and I am a **MORON** for thinking they will and anyone who **DOES** try it on is a **MORON** too.

And so now we are full of **GLOOM** and decide maybe we will just use our expanded brains to help Dad look for his diagram instead.

And that is when something completely **AMAZING** happens, which is that when we get into the office Dad says,

And so we tell him about our **PATENTED BRAIN MASSAGING HELMET** that no one will try on even though it definitely works. But Dad says that in fact **HE** will try it on because he could have been an inventor if he hadn't met Mom, which would mean he would be busy in his laboratory right now making self-boiling eggs instead of looking for drawings of crosswalks, and so we are **PLEASED AS PUNCH**.

So Cosmo squeezes the **PATENTED BRAIN MASSAGING HELMET** on, which is quite tricky, because Dad's head is quite big and the flowerpot is quite small, but in the end Cosmo gives it bang with a book about bees and on it goes, and so does the TV and so does the remote-controlled car. And so Dad is watching

Animal SOS and today it is all about a herd of sheep who have wandered down a cliff and do not know how to wander back again, but a dog named Maurice does and so they **MIRACULOUSLY** do not die and everyone is happy. Except for Dad, because he says it is actually getting a little hot in the helmet, and also a little buzzy and can we take off the whole caboodle because he had better find the crosswalk drawings as the meeting is in half an hour. And I say yes, because now Dad's brain is expanded enough he will remember completely where the crosswalk drawings are so it will be a success all around.

Only it turns out something **UNEXPECTED** has happened, which is that Dad's brain has expanded so **MUCH** that the **PATENTED BRAIN MASSAGING HELMET** will not come off his head at all. In fact, it is completely **STUCK LIKE GLUE**. So Dad says he will cut it off with scissors.

Only Mom says he cannot cut it off with scissors because they are in the **OFF LIMITS** drawer because I glued them together and so they will not work anyway. And then it is clear Dad's brain has expanded because he says some words I have never heard before, but I do not think they are very good ones because Mom says if that is all he can say then he can go straight to his meeting looking like a **MANIAC**, which he does.

And Cosmo can go straight home and not come back until the **HOOPLA** has calmed down, which he does.

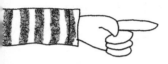

And I can go straight to my room until I have learned that flowerpots and heads **DO NOT MIX**, which I do.

And so I am completely full of gloom because now it is **BACK TO THE DRAWING BOARD** after all and I will not get a hundred thousand dollars or a factory. Daisy says,

But I am **NOT** a **MORON**. And neither is Dad, because it turns out that Mr. O'Flannery liked his idea for coming to the meeting in a helmet representing a traffic jam, and gave him an extra day off at Christmas and so his brain **HAD** expanded after all.

☆ Everybody Loves Penny!

"Penny is an exciting and entertaining character who always has **BRILLIANT IDEAS**... If Penny was my **BFF** then life would never be dull."

Rachel, age 9

"Penny Dreadful stories are very funny and exciting. It is a great series."

Polly, age 10

"I liked Penny because she's naughty, but in a way she's also funny too! I did not like Mrs. Butterworth because she's got a mustache."

Millie, age 8

"I think Penny Dreadful is, well, dreadfully funny. (She sounds a little like my brother — hee hee.) PS I'm turning a little dreadful too."

Islay, age 8

"I think Penny Dreadful is a great book! I learned 'e.g.' means 'for example.' I learned 'i.e.' means 'that is.'"

Bryn, age 8

"A hilariously funny read!"

Anastasia, age 11

"I loved Penny Dreadful, especially in **'PENNY DREADFUL BECOMES A HAIRSTYLIST'**. And the lady with the mustache. Fantastico!"

Leila, age 7

"I love Penny Dreadful, she is brilliant and very funny."

Iona, age 6

"I wanted to read on and on and on...it was soooo good."

Matt, age 8

"This book is funny and full of **BRILLIANT IDEAS** and I like the way it uses '**E.G.**' all the time!"

Megan Emily, age 6

"Here are some of the things I enjoyed about the book:

1. I liked it when Penny and Cosmo tried to shave Barry the cat (the coolest cat ever).
b) Does Penny ever comb her hair?
3. Where did Cosmo get his Jedi suit... I want one!
iv. I liked Mrs. Butterworth at the general store and her mustache!"

Gruffudd, age 10

Joanna Nadin

wrote this book – and lots of others like it. She is small, funny, clever, sneaky and musical. Before she became a writer, she wanted to be a champion ballroom dancer or a jockey, but she was actually a lifeguard at a swimming pool, a radio newsreader, a cleaner in an old people's home, and a juggler. She likes peanut butter on toast for breakfast, and jam on toast for dessert. Her perfect day would involve baking, surfing, sitting in cafes in Paris, and playing with her daughter – who reminds her a lot of Penny Dreadful…

Jess Mikhail

illustrated this book.
She loves creating funny
characters with bright
colors and fancy

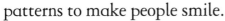

patterns to make people smile.

Her favorite place is her tiny home, where she
lives with her tiny dog and spends lots of time
drawing, scanning, scribbling, printing, stamping,
and sometimes using her scary computer.

She loves to rummage through a good charity shop

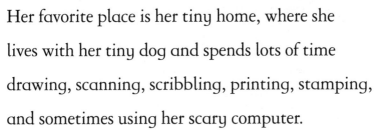

to find weird and wonderful things.

A perfect day for her would have to
involve a sunny beach and large
amounts of spicy foods and ice
cream (not together).

For Millie,
who is always **BRILLIANT™**,
and only sometimes dreadful...

First published in the UK in 2013 by Usborne Publishing Ltd., Usborne House,
83-85 Saffron Hill, London EC1N 8RT, England. www.usborne.com

Copyright © Joanna Nadin, 2013
Illustrations copyright © Usborne Publishing Ltd., 2013

A CIP catalogue record for this book is available from the British Library.

First published in America in 2016 AE.

PB ISBN 9780794535247
ALB ISBN 9781601303707
JFMAMJJA OND/15 02844/9
Printed in Dongguan, Guangdong, China.

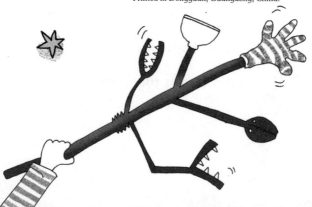